BOVINERUS

JASON TERHUNE
IVANA AGUAYO

Intro:

The state of Nebraska holds some of the greatest beauty that anyone lucky enough to drive through her will ever see. The western half of the state, known as the Bad Lands, is largely filled with sand dunes. It is here that you will find the large flat expanses that many know the state for. This region is filled with many cattle ranches as well as wheat fields. The towns, especially those of any size, are few and far between. A man can drive on a lonely road and not see a single soul for hours; Heaven in many a man's eyes. While some would find this region of the state rather drab, I assure you it holds a beauty all its own. Those who live here are rugged, the descendants of the Native Americans as well as the cowboys of the plains. These folks, both Native and white, hold a direct link to both those born on, as well as those settlers who immigrated there from lands far and wide. Their people lived in teepees and sod houses, homes made of the very wildlife and the land itself. It was their ancestors that put the first plow to the land, taming the ancient soil.

The eastern half of the state is the polar opposite of the western portion. Unlike the west which is largely flat, the eastern portion of the state is defined by beautiful rolling hills. These hills are covered in the many crops that not only feed this nation, but the entire world. Intertwined within these hills one will find small farm after small farm. Like the west, the vast majority of the people of this region can trace their ancestors to both the Native Americans and the many people who immigrated to this region for a chance to own their own land. These people as well are the descendents of those who put the first plows to the soil, the ancestors of those who first tamed a formally wild land.

Unlike the western portion of the state, the eastern portion has ample water sources, there are no bad lands here, only deep dark soil and fresh water. The many creeks flowing through the farmland drain into the powerful Missouri River, the Platte River, and so on. This region also holds the vast bulk of the population for the entire state. Here, unlike in the west, one will find a town every ten miles, as was set up by the railroad nearly one hundred years ago.

If one thing does tie the two sides of the state together, it is the cattle industry. While the west is known for the massive cattle ranches, the eastern section of the state is known for the many feed lots. The cattle are brought in from the western portion of the state to the eastern portion of the state to be held in these lots. The cattle are raised on fresh grass and other plants in the west. They are allowed to grow as big as they can before sending them to the east for slaughter. Once in the east they are sent to the cattle lots. If there is any aspect of the industry that is truly wrong, it is the feed/cattle lot aspect.

The feed lot is the place the cows are all sent just before they are to be slaughtered. It is here where the cow will go from eight hundred pounds to twelve hundred pounds in a matter of a month or two. The cows are fed a super high protein feed with the only goal to add hundreds of pounds to them. The fatter the cow, the fatter the pay off.

Often the unscrupulous feed lot owner will give the cattle shots of random growth hormones. Although many of these hormones are legal, there are plenty that are illegal as well. It was only a matter of time before something terribly wrong would happen. Everyone knew it, yet no one wanted to be the one to say I told you so...

Chapter 1:

Dan Janke had grown up farming his small piece of land just outside of Wayne, Nebraska. His father had farmed this land all his life, as did his father before him. Dan is the third in the line of what his father hoped would be many. Despite this, Dan has never really wanted to be a farmer. He had big hopes and even bigger dreams. He had wanted to move off to New York City and work on Wall Street. Dan had gone to college for economics and is virtually a math wizard.

What are dreams but hopes that were never acted upon? What is a hope, but a dream never realized? Most of us start out with big dreams, we all want to move away from our hometown and make it big. If you play music, you want to move to California and become a rock star. The same goes with anyone in theater that longs to make it in the movies. Yet far too often life just seems to get in the way of our dreams. Obligations to family and those we love often take precedent over one's own hopes, dreams, and desires.

This is what happened with Dan Janke, known as Dan, Dan the Wrecking Man among his small group of friends. While he had wanted

to leave for New York City after he graduated college, fate intervened.
One day while tending the cattle, his father was crossing the road on his
four-wheeler. Out of the blue a truck flew over the hill and smashed into
him. While his father was not killed, nearly every bone in his body was
broken. He had to be flown on the life flight chopper all the way to Sioux
City. During his trip he actually died *three times*, each time being
brought back to life by the paramedics.

Dan knew that he had no choice but to put off his dream of moving to
New York City. Dan was now not just the man of the house but the boss
of the farm. The bright lights of New York City would have to be traded
for the star filled nights of the Nebraska sky as seen from his family
homestead. Now and again, despite one's hopes and dreams, life just
happens. What we do at that moment in time shows the character of a
man. Dan may not like it, but this was his moment. Being the man that
Dan is, the product of a proper Midwest upbringing, not only did he step
up to his obligation, he stood tall. If not for the ability to stand up tall
and proud and help one's family and the ones we love, is there any other
measure of a man?

Chapter 2:

As it does life simply happened, and Dan found himself the manager of a large farm. This being the case and his father out of the way he decided to make all the upgrades and changes that he had always wanted to. While his father was a successful farmer and a steward of the land, he was also very old school. Yet he had made the upgrades to the farm that he had seen fit when he had taken it over from his father. Dan was just following a pattern passed down from generation to generation.

One of Dan's greatest additions to the farm, besides his addition of large windmills, was his herd of prize cattle. No other farmers had the foresight that Dan had. While they kept doing things as they always had for generations, he wasn't about to do the same. His cattle were all considered the American version of Japanese Kobe beef. While the average cow sells for maybe two thousand dollars, Dan's cattle sell for twenty thousand dollars each. His cows are pampered; they have a select diet designed especially for a Kobe cow. The cows are massaged, fed beer as well as special grains. In truth the vast majority of Dan's cattle live better than most people.

All this special treatment is supposed to bring about a much higher quality meat. There are no feed lots in any of these cows' future, unlike virtually every other cow in Nebraska. Much to Dan's dismay, one of those dreaded cattle lots sits just a mile over from his farm. Dan knows all the horrible and dishonest practices that his neighbor used to pack the pounds on his cattle before sending them off for slaughter. If there is anything that he could have ever done he would have; sadly he has no recourse.

His greatest fear is that one day his cows will escape the enclosure of his pasture and mingle with the corrupted cattle of his neighbor. Little does Dan know that his neighbor Shawn has been experimenting with very dangerous new methods to make his cattle grow to unheard of sizes. The things that he is doing over in his barns would make any mad scientist excited.

There is only so much that man should attempt to change. Man longs to improve on everything that he touches, it is our nature. Yet there are some things that we attempt to improve on that come back to bite us in the ass later. Attempting to change the physical make up of an animal is one of these things. Every creature is supposed to evolve on its own timeline. To alter this, to attempt to speed this timeline up, is to play the role of God.

Shawn is nothing like Dan in any way. While Dan looks to be a steward of the land, Shawn wants to control it. Dan sees the land and all of his livestock as something to be worked with, something to respect; Shawn sees it as something to conquer, something to control. If you raise a cow that is eight hundred pounds and you can get two thousand dollars for it, why not figure out a way to make that cow weigh twice as much? Shawn does not believe in any sort of a natural order. He believes in one thing and one thing only, money.

Shawn has no desire to live on some boring ass farm. While most farmers would walk outside and smell the cow manure and say,

"Smells like money."

Shawn will walk outside and say,

"Smells like shit!"

He has never wanted to live on this damn farm, nor had he wanted to take it over when his dad passed away. Shawn has a plan, get rich no matter what the cost, move to Las Vegas, get a nice house with a pool and a little Asian mail order bride.

Chapter 3:

Shawn's barn looks like a scene from countless horror films. Once one has entered this barn, they instantly find themselves asking whether they had just walked onto the set of Saw or Texas Chainsaw Massacre. The difference is that both of those are just sets; Shawn's barn is very real. If not the set of a horror film, it would not be outside the realm of possibility that they have entered the laboratory of some mad scientist. Possibly one will find Frankenstein's monster; Shawn's bulls are not far from that.

Once you enter this barn of death the entire place is covered in long, blood covered plastic strips. In each of the many stalls are cattle in different states of mutation. Looking into these stalls you feel as if you are looking at an old-time freak show. There are cattle with two heads, yet still alive and breathing. There is one cow that has eight legs like a spider. There are a few cross-bred species between cattle and hogs.

Shawn has even dabbled in human/cow experiments, using his own DNA to mix with the bovine DNA.

There is yet one other part of the barn that Shawn uses to *create,* if you will. Life as a farmer is not easy in this day and age, especially for the small farmer. Unlike his neighbor Dan Janke, Shawn is just not that smart, at least not where business is concerned. Dan saw the future and rented portions of his land out for windmills for energy creation. These windmills alone make Dan more money in one month than Shawn makes from his entire farm in a year. This, combined with his pampered Kobe cows which bring twenty times the price of one of Shawn's cows, means Dan is set. All Shawn can do is look over at Dan's place and say,

"To Hell with that son of a bitching Dan."

Shawn had been forced; at least that's how he sees it. This has led to him having to find money via other means. While Shawn knows that corn and beef may not always sell well, Meth will *always* sell. This being the case, Shawn decided to take his vast knowledge of chemistry and put it to work. Miss. Zobel had taught him well in High School chemistry class. Shawn is not only making meth; Shawn is working on his own version of a super meth. He knows that if he can make the best meth, he can corner the local market and make as much money and as fast as he can. In theory his idea is not only sound but a great one. Just like his neighbor Dan has done with cattle Shawn plans to do with meth. The money that he will make from his first batches of meth will go towards his research into making his super meth.

Shawn is in his lair, his inner sanctum, off limits to everyone but him and his brother Dusty. It is this area, his inner sanctum, where the meth is made. So far, the batches that he and Dusty have made have been really good, yet they are not anywhere near the level that Shawn desires. The brothers are in a race against time to make their batch of super meth and corner the market, especially now. Recently the Mexican cartels have moved into the area. They have moved in from Omaha and Sioux City, flooding the area with high grade and extremely cheap meth. The brothers know that if they don't have a breakthrough soon, not only will their wealth be at stake but possibly their lives. One thing that everyone knows on either side of the border, if you value your head being attached to your body, do not get in the cartel's way.

Dusty enters the makeshift area of the barn where his brother Shawn is working away. He won't tell his brother, but he is appalled at the sights that he sees. His brother's experiments make him sick. Despite this he supports his brother either way, that is what family does. Dusty knows that it is only a matter of time before Shawn makes the breakthrough that they both need. Let Shawn play with his cattle; the meth is where the money is, Dusty thinks to himself. Dusty could not care less about the cattle, he only cares about the meth. Farming has never been his thing, nor will it be. That is the world of his brother and his late father. Shawn just wants one big score, sell it all and get out of the business; not Dusty though. After just selling three batches of meth Dusty now sees himself much like a Scarface figure, the Scarface of the Midwest. To hell with making a larger cow, only one thing matters, making a stronger meth. All the cow mutation shit, well that makes Dusty want to puke in his mouth. If his father was still alive, he would beat his brother's ass and kick him off the farm. His father, unlike him or his brother, was a steward of the land, a man of honor, and a real Nebraska farmer.

Dusty knows that the drug life isn't for Shawn. Let him make his breakthrough, then he takes over, Dusty thinks over and over again. Let Shawn have his dream of moving to Las Vegas and getting his little house with a pool and a mail order bride from the Philippines. He may be the one who makes the shit, but he is far from the brains of the operation.

Chapter 3:

"Hey big brother what do you have cooking up in here?"

"You are fucking late Dusty. You were supposed to be here damn near an hour ago. You know that this shit is dangerous to work with, especially alone. At any given moment all it will take is one wrong movement and this whole place will blow sky high."

"So let me get this straight...you want me here so that if you get blown to Kingdom Come I get to blow up with you? You want me here so that if this shit blows, I get blown to pieces, burned alive, or turned into some hideous deformed monster? All so you don't die alone?"

"It is just easier to have two damn people Dusty. I need to have someone to double check each move I make for safety purposes. Now put your damn ventilator on; the fumes in this place will kill you or rot what's left of that damn brain of yours."

"How is this batch looking big brother? That last batch was good. I would say as good if not better than any of the Mexican shit flooding the area. We just need to make a batch that is even stronger. If we do this, we will make twice as much money off of the same size batch."

"That is what I have been saying about making a bigger cow. You never listened to me then, this is the same damn thing little brother."

"I am not you Shawn, and I am not Dad. I don't give a shit about those or any cows, let alone this damn farm. That batch of meth right there, that is our future, not some goddamn mutant cow."

"If the old man heard you say that he would roll over in his grave."

"Well that is exactly where he is, in his grave. That means that I am no longer beholden to him or his old-fashioned ways. In fact, neither are you big brother. If Dad saw the shit that you are doing in this barn with these mad scientist experiments and mutant cattle, he would kick your ass."

"Enough about Dad and about what he would or would not do. I think that I have figured out the recipe for your fabled batch of super meth."

"How so big brother?"

"The other day I was in the Co-Op store. I bought us a huge batch of fertilizer that had been recalled. According to old man Tom the batch was supposed to be sent back to Monsanto. Tom told me not only did the shit make the crops grow two and three times the size, it made one hell of a batch of meth as well. I guess the shit worked too good, can't let the people make anything extra. Tom also told me some bullshit story about how he had heard the fertilizer was made with nuclear waste over in China. Toxic waste or not he said he tried some meth made from it and it was the best that he ever had. He gave me damn near a ton of the shit for next to nothing and an ounce of meth when its cooked up."

"Well shit Shawn, you have my ear big brother."

"The only problem Dusty is damn does this shit stink. I am afraid that making this batch will stink so damn bad that even the stench of the feed lot won't hide it. I don't want that son of a bitch Dan to stick his nose where it don't belong, let alone call the damn law."

"That fool won't do shit Shawn. Hell, right now he is probably having sex with one of those prize cows of his."

"You're right little brother, fuck that guy and his stupid ass cows and windmills. You know I heard Trump say that those windmills cause cancer; I bet there is something to that."

"Well if Trump says it then it must be true. Probably all a part of Dan's liberal agenda, give us all cancer and then take our land. Goddamn liberals, if it's not one thing it's another."

The two brothers work into the night mixing up their batch of super meth. Finally, after around four hours of cooking up their batch they are finished. As the brothers look at the meth, which has an odd green tint to it, they do so almost scared. They both know that one of them has to be the test dummy for what may be their new super product.

"So Shawn you are older so that means you get to go first right?"

"Fuck that shit Dusty; you are the one that does drugs in the damn first place. I am more than happy with a cold beer and a joint. I hate this damn shit."

"Okay let's make a compromise. We will both do it okay? How is that, you cool with that big brother?"

"Yeah I am cool with that man."

Shawn takes a small piece of the crystal they had just made and smashes it down into a powder. He then cuts the powder into two lines, one for him and one for his brother to snort.

Chapter 4:

Shawn leans down and snorts up the first line. When he comes up from doing so he looks as if he has just been possessed by the Devil himself. His entire face turns tomato red and his eyes look as if they are about to pop out of their very sockets. Inside of his body he can feel each and every one of his atoms burst to life. It is as if they are a part of a car's fuel system that has just been ignited.

Dusty looks at his brother in shock and awe. Looking at his brother is making him think twice about trying his line. The line that Shawn just took was half of the size of either of their normal lines. Dusty looks at his brother thinking, if this meth just did this to Shawn how damn strong is this shit?

"Are you sure that I should try this Shawn? No offense but you look like you are possessed or are a mad man!"

"You have to try this shit Dusty."

"Okay if you say so but I am going on record as saying that this may be a bad idea."

Dusty leans down and snorts up the entirety of his line. In an instant he feels as if his nose is on fire. It feels as if his entire body is a large pack of Black Cat firecrackers whose fuse has just been lit. A normal line of meth makes you feel as if you are going one hundred miles an hour while standing still. This, this single line makes you feel as if you are going hyper sonic speeds while standing still. Dusty looks up from his line at his brother,

"I think that I have just seen the face of god big brother."

"Well then, I say that we do some more little brother."

The two brothers snort line after line until they feel as if their hearts may actually explode. That or they will suffer a massive stroke from the insane quality of this batch of meth. Out of the blue Shawn seems to go crazy and runs out of the room. Dusty quickly runs out into the barn after his brother.

"Fuck these cows! Fuck this farm! I just want to head out to Vegas, get my little mail order bride and live my own life."

Shawn runs up to one of his largest creations. Inside of this pen is a bull that weighs close to three thousand pounds; the average bull is maybe half this size. Shawn's creation may as well have come from some ancient long-lost age.

"Fuck you, you son of a bitching Bull!"

"Yeah what Shawn said; fuck you cow!"

"I am going to let this thing out of its pen and kill it little brother. You are right Dusty I am not dad and I will never be him!"

"You are right big brother let that son of a bitch out and let's make steaks out of its ass."

Blasted on super meth and having no clue what it is that they are doing, as well as any idea the enormity of the mistake that they are making, Shawn opens up the mutant bull's pen. In an instant the massive abomination of God charges out of the pen with the fury of Hell. Doing what only a man blasted on meth would do, Shawn attempts to attack the bull. In an instant the mutant bull rears up with one of its massive horns. The bull swerves its head and skewers Shawn through the chest with the entire length of its horn. The bull then begins to shake and twist its body, launching Shawn's body up in the air then catching it again and again.

Dusty is standing in utter shock, not even able to move. Shawn's body is spewing blood in all directions as the massive bull toys with him like a cat with a mouse. Dusty is covered in his brother's blood along with the walls of the barn.

"No Shawn, No!"

In an instant the massive mutant bull turns around and kicks Dusty in the chest. When he is hit by the two large hooves it is with the force of a Mack Truck going eighty miles an hour. He flies through the air smashing against the far wall of the barn. Just before joining his brother and father in the afterlife, Dusty watches the massive mutant bull begin to kick down the walls of all of the other stalls, letting loose its mutant brothers and sisters. With his last breath Dusty laughs remembering watching South Park with his brother and the immortal words of Mr. Mackey,

"Drugs are bad ummkay."

Chapter 5:

The mutant cattle, now all free, begin to walk around the barn. Finally, the mutant bull following its nose finds the batch of super meth. All the other cattle follow their now leader into the lab with the meth. The mutant bull sniffs the super meth and looks at the other cattle puzzled. He then leans down with the other cattle and begins eating the super meth. Instantly the bull along with the other cattle begin to go insane and fall to the ground.

Like with Shawn and Dusty the meth has much the same effect on the cattle's bodies. Like the brothers their bodies feel as if they are going to explode from the rush of adrenaline that is running through them. They begin to feel each and every atom in their bodies begin to explode with a fire so hot it could be on the very sun. Yet unlike Shawn and Dusty who had not had massive amounts of experiments done on them, the meth begins to cause instant side effects in the bodies of the cattle. Being made from Chinese nuclear waste the fertilizer used to make the meth held unknown properties. Shawn had been told by old man Tom that this fertilizer had made the crops grow to unheard of sizes.

This toxic waste-based meth shot like lightning through the already mutant cows' bodies. Instantly they all fell to the ground. With deafening screams the cattle all writhed to and fro on the ground. All the cattle were now growing to three times and more their previous sizes. Along with this something even scarier began to happen. Where a normal cow has flat teeth for grinding grasses and grains these cows now all grew long sharp fangs. The cattle are now carnivores.

The newly mutated cattle now complete in their mutation begin to rip apart the bodies of both Shawn and his brother Dusty. They tear chunks of flesh from the bodies. They devour flesh and even bone as if it is as soft as butter. Their long fangs are the perfect tools for tearing apart the flesh of anything that crosses their path. The bodies now devoured, the cattle all follow the mutant bull as it crashes through the side of the barn and out into the field. The once three-thousand-pound mutant bull is now easily twice that size, and standing nearly twenty feet tall.

Chapter 6:

Dan felt safe letting his prize herd graze in his pasture that night. The news had said that the weather was going to be perfect, a rare thing for the North East Nebraska. Not to mention Dan had moved the herd to the west side of the pasture. While this side stunk a bit due to his idiot neighbors feed lot it was filled with all-natural green prairie grass.

One of the things about raising Kobe beef is that they not only eat all natural but only eat the best. The grass in that field has never seen a single chemical. In fact, Dan personally spread the seed and manure in that field for the past two years. The seeds that he planted are ancient grass seeds that are native to this very region of Nebraska. It brought him great joy and honor looking out over his fields. Knowing that his field looks the same as it did hundreds of years ago strengthened his tie to the land.

Dan has no clue what has been going down on his neighbors' farm. He had long ago quit caring about the actions of Shawn or his idiot brother Dusty. As long as nothing they did affected him, his herd, or his land what they do is their business, not his. As always, he suspects that they are up to no good. Once again though, this is none of his business. Dan simply figures that eventually whatever it is they are doing over there will all be exposed to the light of the day. Wayne is a small town, as well are all the other small communities in the region. In these parts word spreads fast, and rumors spread even faster. In fact, plenty of rumors have already began to find their way into the different circles around Wayne.

Secretly Dan hopes that all the rumors are true. If the rumors are true and the brothers are cooking up drugs Dan sees only two outcomes. First, the idiot brothers will blow themselves up cooking that poison and die. Second, they will get busted and end up down in Lincoln in prison for god knows how many years. As far as Dan is concerned either outcome works for him; both lead to a positive outcome for him. Despite which way it goes for the brothers Dan will be able to buy their land cheap. This will allow him to finally get rid of that disgusting feed lot and its horrific stench. It is all just a matter of time he thinks. Dusty proving just how much of an idiot he is has been bragging around town about his new venture. Word travels fast; it is a given that the law already knows what he is up to.

With no clue as to what has just transpired at his neighbors' farm, Dan is home asleep in his bed. Dan had a long day of work on the farm and was beat when he was done. In his world sleep is a luxury, as it is for each and every farmer worldwide. It is said that the life of a farmer is from sunup until sun down. This is a lie though, just a gesture meant to glorify the life of the farmer. On an average day Dan is up hours before sunrise and rarely stops working until long after sundown. Unlike the average man who works his forty hours a week Dan works twice that. Not to mention the fact that he works seven days a week, the cattle don't stop eating on the weekends. It is said that there is no rest for the wicked. The real truth is that there is no rest for the American farmer.

As the mutant cattle rush from the barn they run out into the fields. These cattle are no longer anything representing a normal cow any longer though. As they run through the field the toxic waste running through their veins is still causing new and even scarier mutations. All their once flat teeth are now long and yellow fangs. Where once they longed for fresh green grass, now they long for only the taste of blood and the feel of flesh in their mouths. There's a strange neon green goo dripping profusely from their mouth and fangs. Even their eyes have an eerie green glow from the radioactivity encompassing their bodies.

As the mutant cattle race through the fields they make a horrific screaming noise. To hear this is to hear a thousand banshees all screaming at once. The mutant herd smashes through the simple barbwire fence separating Dan's land from Shawn's. Worse of all the only thing that is separating Dan's prize herd from Shawn's land.

In an instant the mutant herd attacks Dan's prize cattle. They begin to bite and tear into the flesh of the Kobe beef. Yet rather than tear them to shreds they only bite the cattle randomly. All of those bitten begin to fall down upon the pasture floor. Blood now covers the once green prairie grass. The prize herd writhes in pain as the mutant saliva and goo now run through their veins, infecting them with their horrific illness. Like Shawn's mutant cattle Dan's herd now begin to grow to twice their former size. Their teeth now grow into large fangs, dripping the toxic neon green goo. Every one of Dan's previously prized herd are now infected with the radioactive Bovinerus.

Chapter 7:

Now all mutated, Dan's infected cattle rise from the ground. Before they had all been docile, content to lounge and eat the prairie grass that Dan had diligently planted just for them all day and night. Now, just like their mutant creators, they long only for blood and flesh. Suddenly they pick up the scent of flesh in the air. Just behind Dan's house is a small pig enclosure. This is where Dan keeps his twenty prize hogs. Like his cattle these hogs are all organic. The flesh of these swine is sweeter than any pork found in all of America. It is this delicious scent that the mutant herd picks up on the gentle winds over the fields.

Now all connected via a mental connection the mutant herd move as one as it rushes towards Dan's prize hogs. As they move, their screaming is so loud that surely it would have awoken any other man, but not Dan. Dan is no normal man; before he fell into his bed, he had put in an eighteen hour day. As well he had fallen asleep while his favorite Dead Kennedys album is playing on repeat. Between his utter exhaustion and the soothing sound of Jello Biafra's voice, Dan may as well be dead to the world.

As the mutant herd smashes through the walls of the hog enclosure it is as loud as a bomb going off. The mutant herd begin tearing the hogs to pieces, ripping legs and chunks of flesh from the screaming hogs. Between the sound of the destruction of the hog confinement, the screaming mutant cattle, and the shrieks of the hogs being torn to pieces Dan jumps up from his sleep. He instantly flips on his bedroom light and just stands there for a second listening.

"What the hell is going on?"

In a state of shock Dan throws his boots on, grabs his AK-47 from the gun rack above his bed and rushes outside to investigate. He instantly hits the switch that turns all of the lights on the homestead portion of the farm on. Like a soldier running into battle Dan rushes towards his prize hog enclosure. Instantly he is shocked at what it is that he is witnessing. He can't believe his eyes as he watches his own prize herd tear apart his hogs. Two of the mutant herd are fighting over one of the hog's entrails, like two dogs over a rope. The mutants are tearing through the bodies of the other hogs biting down like a swarm of sharks on a dead whale. Blood covers the floor and walls of what is left of the enclosure. Dan is lost; he has been a farmer all of his life and has never heard of, let alone *seen*, anything like what is going on before his very eyes.

"What in the name of all that is sacred and holy?"

When Dan looks at the cows more closely, he notices the changes that has come over them. Each cow is now twice their normal size, has long fangs, and those eyes, those eerie eyes. He is lost in his own head; everything that he has ever known is now upside down. He need only take one look at these cows to know that something was far from right. Just then one of Dan's prize cows, his favorite of the herd Yolondi, takes notice of him. Dan had personally fed this cow beer with a giant bottle on countless occasions. Normally his mere presence would bring Yolondi by his side. The cow had taken to following him like a dog or a small child.

Now this once formally prized cow is looking at Dan with evil infused into its veins. As she looks at Dan Yolondi begins to snort and smash her foot down on to the ground. As she does this, she stares at Dan looking at him with her green glowing eyes and green saliva dripping from her long yellow fangs. In an instant like a bat out of hell she rushes Dan screaming as she does so. Not knowing what to do Dan turns around and runs as fast as he can towards the house. Against all odds he is able to outrun the mutant beast and slams the door shut to his home.

Dan lands on his ass and back as he flies into the house. As the door is slammed Yolondi begins to crash through it, tearing it to shreds. Her head now through the door Dan is staring in disbelief at what is transpiring before his very eyes. He yells out.

"Yolondi, Yolondi it's me, Daddy. Be a good girl Yolondi."

His pleas with the mutant cow go unheard, falling upon deaf ears. Now the beast begins to smash through the door frame and into the house. Knowing there is no other option Dan unloads into the face of his once prize Kobe cow with his AK-47. The bullets do as they are designed and tear through the skull of the mutant cow. Pieces of brain matter, skull, and blood cover Dan along with the walls of his home. He quickly flips the magazine and allows all thirty shells to blast through the cow's skull. Finally, Yolondi the mutant cow drops dead onto the ground. As soon as this happens the entire herd stops and screams in unison knowing through their mental connection that they had lost one of their own.

Chapter 8:

Dan quickly grabs five loaded magazines of ammo and makes his way up onto the roof of his house. As he looks out over the mutant herd Dan watches them tearing off in the direction of the town of Wayne, just eight miles away. As he looks down onto the ground, he sees random chunks of flesh that used to be his hogs. Small potholes that would normally be filled with water are now filled with blood and green radioactive goo.

Knowing that only two people will ever believe him as to what has just happened, Dan looks down at his phone. There is no real point in calling the police, he thinks to himself. At best they would think that he is drunk or high on whacky Tabacky. They may possibly think that he is on some of that shit that Shawn and his brother are cooking up. No this will have to be taken care of by him and his own people. Despite whether they will believe him or not Dan decides that he has to let the town cops know. Even if they don't believe him maybe, just maybe they will warn the town. Looking down at his phone with shaky fingers he types in 911. As the phone begins to ring, Dan really isn't sure just what it is that he is even going to say.

"911, you have reached the Wayne Municipal Police Department. How can I help you?"

Dan, not even able to control himself, lets everything out to the operator.

"You have to act quick. There is a mutant herd of cattle heading towards Wayne right now! They have already killed my hogs. My prize cow Yolondi almost killed me before I killed her. I had to unload on her with my AK-47."

"Dan, Dan Janke is that you?"

"Yes, yes this is Dan!"

"Dan it's me Mandy. Now what the hell is going on? Are you okay? You didn't take any sort of drugs, did you? Are you drunk?"

"No, I am not drunk and no I am not on any fucking drugs! I am telling you that there is a herd of mutant flesh-eating cattle heading towards Wayne right now! You have to alert the town. I don't know how long they will take to get to you, but they are heading your way right now. You need to tell everyone before it's too late."

"Dan, we go back all the way before High School. This is the only reason that I am not going to tell any of the guys on duty that you are obviously high out of your mind. Now hang up, go to bed and sleep whatever you are on off."

With that Mandy hangs up the phone. Dan just laughs to himself as he looks at his phone.

"I bet that I sounded like a real nut job to Mandy. I don't blame her I wouldn't believe me either, how could anyone?"

Dan knows that everything is up to him now. He knew that there are only two people that he can call. These two men have been his brothers his entire life. Not only will the two of them believe him, they are both armed to the teeth. Even better they are always willing to go to war. He looks down at his phone and types in the one number that he knows that has never changed, 402-375-2154. This number belongs to only one man,

Travis Posvar. As the phone rings Dan tries to think of just what he is going to say.

"Hey what's up Dan, this is crazy late for you. What's going on bro? It must be important for you to call this late."

"Bro you are not going to believe me, but my herd of cows have mutated. I think that my neighbor Shawn's herd has joined them. Maybe it is the other way around, I don't know."

"Whoa Dan slow down bro. Now what the fuck are you talking about?"

"Dude the goddamn things have fangs now. They are twice their normal size and they now eat fucking flesh. They tore apart my hogs and fucking ate them man. I had to kill Yolondi. The damn thing broke down my door trying to kill and eat me. I dumped two thirty round magazines from my AK into her head before she dropped. This shit is fucking real man. Even worse the mutant herd is heading right towards Wayne as we speak.

"They are heading here?"

"Yes, Travis they are heading to Wayne as we speak."

"Dan you know that I love you bro. Are you sure that you didn't drink or smoke anything?"

"I so wish that was the case Travis. No, this shit is real. It is up to us bro; we have to kill these sons a bitches ourselves. I tried to call the cops. Mandy wouldn't put me through; damn girl hung up on me."

"Typical man, fucking cops. So, what is up with the cows? Do you know what turned them into mutants?"

"How the hell should I know? Some sort of Bovinerus I suppose. It doesn't matter how this happened; all that matters is that we kill them now. Call Smalley and gather up the guns. I am on my way now."

Chapter 9:

Dan gets off his roof and runs downstairs. Once he is in his room, he quickly throws on all his Real Tree gear. He then loads his many pockets in the hunting coat with as many loaded magazines as he can. It took a lot of ammo to take down Yolondi; it will take a miracle to take down the entire herd. There is no choice though. It is either try to kill as many as they can or end up human burgers for a mutant cow. The key is to save as many lives as possible.

Dan looks at himself in the mirror, he is ready for war. He can't help but take another look.

"Damn you are one sexy son of a bitch. It is no surprise that you see more ass than a toilet seat in a women's public restroom."

With his AK-47, a forty-five on each hip, all the ammo he can carry, and his trusty survival knife, Dan is ready for war. As he walks out of his front door, he takes one last look at his formally prize Kobe cow Yolondi. He is amazed at just what it is that he is looking at. Where the brain is normally pink this cow's brain is an odd green color. As well rather than the normal red blood, all Yolondi's blood is a deep green and has an odd consistency. Dan looks down at his former Bovine friend.

"I don't know what happened to you Yolondi but I am glad that I put you down. I know that you would have never wanted to live like this. I hope that you are eating grass in that big pasture up in the sky. May you one day become a delicious steak for God up in Heaven."

Now ready for battle Dan runs out to his car and jumps in. He turns the key and feels the roar of the engine. As he gets to the bottom of the lane, he smashes his foot down on the gas pedal. The wheels start to spin sending smoke up into the air. As the car hits one hundred miles an hour, Bad Religion pumping through the stereo speakers, he places his hand on the dashboard. The mighty Glurphin, as she has always been known, has never once let him down.

"One more hell ride baby girl. Only on this hell ride baby, we are not trying to outrun a Centaur like that night with Kristen and Jason coming home from Norfolk. God speed old friend, god speed oh mighty Glurphin."

Dan makes the eight-mile drive in a matter of minutes. He races to the one place that he knows is safe, at least for the moment, Travis' house. Once there he ramps the mighty Glurphin over the curb and onto the yard. Travis instantly comes out of the house.

"Dude my dad is going to be pissed. Look what you did to the yard?"

"There is no time for this crap Travis. They may have already reached the town for all I know. Did you call Smalley?"

"Yeah he just got done unloading everything into the house."

"Good man, good let's get back into the house before it's too late."

The old friends rush into Travis' house. This house has been considered a safe place all their lives. Smalley meets the two in the living room.

"What the hell is going on Dan? Travis said you were talking about mutant killer cows?"

"Yeah Smalley I was. I have no clue as to how but my herd, along with Shawn's next door, are all mutated now. The damn things have green glowing eyes, fucking long yellow fangs, they are twice their former size. Oh, and last but not least, because why not, they are now carnivorous. I don't know how or why this has happened other than maybe God is playing a joke on us? Who knows maybe the Hindu cow god has finally decided to strike back for all I know? What I do know Smalley, is that this is real and that goddamn mutant herd is on its way here as we speak. If it isn't already here."

"You know Dan, this all kind of makes odd sense."

"Please tell me how the hell any of this makes sense Smalley, because brother I am at a loss here."

"Well I have been hearing a lot of rumors around town that Shawn and his brother Dusty picked up a shitload of fertilizer. What I heard around the Co-Op is that it was all supposed to be destroyed. The Old Man told me that it was supposed to be corrupted and made from Chinese nuclear waste. I guess there were issues with the batch worldwide. Of course, our government and the Chinese have covered it all up. Yet despite destroying most of the fertilizer I guess a bit slipped through the cracks. Shawn just happened to get ahold of some. I hear tell he and Dusty were trying to make some sort of super meth with it. I'm guessing that the cattle got into the toxic waste fertilizer somehow and that is what has mutated them all."

"Well Smalley as I see it, nuclear waste, mutant cattle, some bizarre Bovinerus, none of that matters now. All that matters now brother is that we kill each and every one of these mutant sons a bitches."

Chapter 10:

"Now Travis show me what we are working with."

"Dan, we are ready for war. I have AR-15's for all of us. I see that you have your AK, but you may as well take this as well. Like you, our side arms are forty fives. I also have a case of hand grenades and then of course there is this...this my brother, this is a missile launcher. This little girl will shoot four big ass firecrackers. If this baby can't take down a mutant cow, nothing can. So how do you like those apples, Danny boy?"

"I like those apples indeed; I like those apples indeed my brother."

"Oh and Dan?"

"Yeah Smalley?"

"We have a truck that I have been working on. My thirty-eight Ford four by four. Oh yeah, she has one hell of a cattle catcher on her as well. I am calling her the Death Pod."

Dan looks out of the window. In his rush to get to Travis' house, he hadn't even taken notice of the bad ass truck in the driveway.

"Now that is one hell of a machine Smalley. I have always said that if it has wheels and a motor, Smalley can make it bad to the fucking bone."

What Dan, Travis, and Smalley didn't know is that the mutant cows now have the ability to run over thirty miles an hour. Since the herd had escaped Dan's farm, they have all been running towards Wayne. Along the way they took out three different farms, killing everyone and everything not in the bovine family. Along with their killing spree they have also infected nearly one hundred other cows. This is now not a mutant herd; this is now a mutant bovine Army.

Out of the blue Travis' police scanner goes off.

"Quick, quick you have to help me. They, they are mutant cattle, they are everywhere. Get here now I am up by the Pac -N- Save. Oh my god they are rushing the apartments! Even more are running across the street towards the new houses. Help us, God help us!"

The guys all listen as the officer screams as the mutant cattle rip him apart, all with his mic still open. Only the sounds of flesh being torn from his body along with the crush of breaking bones in the fanged mouths of the mutant cattle broke through his screams.

"Holy shit this is fucking real Dan! I almost hoped that you were just having some sort of a breakdown."

"You and me both Travis, you and me both."

"Well guys it looks as if it is up to us then. Travis, Smalley we always knew it would be up to us to save this damn town one day. Let's do this."

The three brothers from other mothers run out of the house. They jump into Smalley's bad ass truck, the Death Pod. Smalley slams his foot down onto the gas. The group flies up the road heading towards Pac-N-Save. As they do so much of the town and people of Wayne are already being attacked and eaten alive. As they drive, the three witness two cows working together to rip a woman in half. Smalley slaps down on a switch on his dashboard. Instantly a giant cattle catcher that he has fashioned in his garage slams down over the grill. This cattle catcher has two-foot-long razor sharp spikes ready to kill anything that crosses its path.

"Holy hell Smalley what did you make this for?"

"Well Dan I like to be ready for anything. Be glad I did make this bad ass MOFO! I told you that this truck was bad ass."

Smalley yells this as he rams the cattle catcher into one of the massive cows. Instantly the body, or at least half of the body, flies up over the top of the truck and on to the ground behind them.

"Oh shit, look over there! Is that Mandy Erickson?"

"Well it was Mandy; what is left of her, anyway."

Smalley hits another cow and it is writhing every which way in the front of the truck. Dan hangs out of the window and begins shooting the mutant cow in the head. After about ten rounds from his AK-47, the cow falls to the ground dead. At that same moment a horrific screaming fills the air as all the mutant herd call out for the loss of one of their own.

"They are like zombies; you have to shoot them in the head to kill them. Travis, get on the radio and get the word out."

"Everyone who can hear this. People of Wayne if you want to kill the mutant cattle you must shoot them in the head. Aim for their eyes; they need a bullet straight to the brain. Shoot them in the fucking head!"

Travis grabs the wheel and Smalley now hangs out the window taking out as many mutant cattle as he can. With only less than ten bullets he drops two of the bastards. The small Nebraska town sounds like a damn war zone. All over the town you can hear the screams of the mutant cattle, the sounds of gun shots being fired, and of course the screams of the townspeople.

Chapter 11:

The guys race through the streets of Wayne trying to kill as many of the cattle as possible. They find themselves smashing the truck into the yard of one of the local sorority houses. Mutant cows are tearing many of the girls apart. The girls that are left are running around frantically, scared for their own lives. Much to the guys' surprise and liking, most of the girls are wearing little to nothing at all.

"Holy shit guys look at all of these hot ass semi naked girls. If we save them all we are guaranteed to get laid."

"Damn right Travis. That sounds like some sound ass logic to me right there. What say you Smalley?"

"I am down with saving and banging out hot college girls seven days a week brother, and twice on Sunday. Let's do this shit."

The three brothers jump out of their truck and begin to blast as many mutant cows in the head as they can.

"Get the fuck upstairs ladies. The mutant cows can't make it up the stairs."

"Thank you, guys, so much. Not only are the three of you our big strong saviors you are our heroes as well."

As the ladies all run up the stairs, Dan, Travis, and Smalley pump as many shells into the mutant cows' brains as they can. Two of the mutants crash into the house taking out the door and the door frame.

"Run Smalley the damn thing is up your ass."

"I got you guys."

Travis takes out the mutant cow with a shot straight to the eye, ripping through its brain. Like a lunatic, Dan jumps onto the back of the other mutant cow and grabs it by the horns. He rides the damn thing like a bucking bronco in the Wayne County Rodeo. Travis, Smalley, and all the girls watch and cheer Dan on as he rides the bull through the house. Dan pulls out his trusty survival knife and rams it into the skull of the bull, clear down into its brain. Instantly the cow drops to the ground like a one-thousand-pound bag of shit.

"Holy shit Dan that was fucking awesome."

"You don't grow up on a farm and not know how to ride a bull brother."

"Well Dan the closest that I have ever come to riding a bull was a big girl named Kendra from Wakefield."

As the guys run through the house, they come across a freshly tapped keg of beer still on ice.

"Holy shit it's a keg of beer. Quick grab my feet."

Travis goes directly into a keg stand as Dan and Smalley grab his legs and hold them up in the air. As he does this, the beautiful sorority girls cheer him on. Having had his fill of cold beer, Travis drops down from what would easily be a record holding time for a keg stand, most likely a world record.

"Oh my god thank you guys so much. You are all my heroes, our knights in shining camo. If there is anything any of us can do for you, or *to* you, to pay you back for saving our lives, well just stop by. We would all be happy to repay you by doing anything that you want."

As she said this the gorgeous half naked sorority girl gave a seductive smile as she bit down on the tip of her finger. The guys all smiled at each other looking at all the hot college girls. Finally, Dan spoke up.

"Ladies I assure you that we will be back. Now take those perfect asses of yours upstairs. The cattle are too heavy to walk up the stairs without breaking them. Now get your sugar tits up those stairs ladies."

With that the college girls ran upstairs and hid in their separate rooms. The guys couldn't wait to come back. If there is anything worth living for it is a house of sex craved, beautiful, horny college girls who only long to please the men who just saved their lives. "Merica," Dan says as he looks over at Travis.

"Bro grab that keg and throw it in the back of the truck. I have an idea."

"That's what I am talking about brother."

"No Travis it's not for what you think."

The guys jump into the truck.

"Smalley, floor this bad ass beast of a machine and get us to Seventh and Main."

The center of town.

Chapter 12:

"Dan, why the hell do you want me to drive you to Seventh and Main?"

"I have an idea, Smalley. I have been feeding these cattle beer nearly every day since they have been calves. I am certain that they are all mentally connected somehow. I am thinking that they must have some sort of leader, a huge bull most likely. I think that if we spray beer into one of the mutant cows' mouths that this will trigger them all to come running for some beer. Then when we see the head bull, we make steaks out of his ass."

"Well that sounds like a waste of a lot of good beer to me Dan."

"Actually, Travis this may just be the best use of beer ever, possibly even save mankind."

"How will we know which one of the bulls is the lead bull controlling all the others?"

"Don't worry about that Smalley. I assure you that we will know, oh we will know. Right now, just do what you do best, drive brother, drive."

Smalley races towards the center of the town of Wayne. Travis is perched of the side of the truck shooting as many of the mutant cows as he can. Cow after cow drops as Travis takes them out with pinpoint precision. It takes one hell of a shot to take out the eyeball of a bull in the back of a bouncing truck driving over fifty miles an hour. These are the types of shots that only Travis could ever make. Cow after mutant cow drops as the brothers make their way to Seventh and Main. Dan looks out of the window and yells to Travis,

"Leave a few for me brother."

The men laugh at Dan's request. Even in a moment such as this it is always nice to find a moment of humor. Once at the center of town Smalley races into the parking lot of the old 7-11, now a car lot.

"Okay guys let's get up onto the roof. I used to work here back in the day; I know where the ladder is to get up top. Help me carry this damn keg of beer up here as well."

Dan, Travis, and Smalley all run around the back of the 7-11. They quickly grab the ladder and begin to rush up to the roof. Travis and Dan are the first onto the roof. They struggle but manage to get the keg of beer up on the roof with them. Finally, Smalley starts to climb the ladder.

"Come on Smalley, get up here man."

"I'm coming guys; I am coming."

Just then one of the mutant cows comes out of nowhere. It sees Smalley and, in a blood and flesh craving rage, it races towards him.

Just before he can get up to the top the mutant cow smashes into the ladder.

"Jump Smalley! Jump!"

Smalley jumps from the ladder and through the air. Dan reaches out and just in time catches Smalley's hand.

"Quick Travis help me pull him up."

Once on the safety of the roof Smalley and the guys look down at the mutant cow. The cow is in a blind rage, smashing its head into the walls of the building. As it does the entire building shakes.

"Holy shit that damn thing is insane. Look at it smashing its head into the brick wall."

"Insane Smalley, they are zombie cows in a rage with one thing on their minds, tearing apart and eating your flesh. Thus, you are correct; that cow is fucking insane!"

"Oh snap look at that cow's ear tag. You see that logo? That is my great grandfather's old brand. You see the capital T, the diamond, and the bar going under the two? That's one of my cows. This is absolutely perfect. Travis bring that keg of beer over here and pump the tap."

Travis and Smalley begin pumping the tap on the keg of beer. While doing this they bring the keg of beer to the edge of the roof. Dan grabs the beer tap and gets ready to fire as the guys pump the tap.

"Hey, you son of a bitching cheeseburger! Look up here!"

The moment that mutant cow looks up with its mouth open and its fangs exposed, Dan shoots a steady stream of beer directly into its mouth. The guys all look at each other, not quite sure what, if anything, is about to happen. Instantly the mutant cow stops in its tracks and lets out one of the loudest screams any of the guys have ever heard. The guys all look at each other again not quite sure just what is about to happen but ready for anything.

Chapter 13:

In an instant the entire town of Wayne feels as if it has just fallen victim to a five-point earthquake. The cow that ingested the beer must have sent out a mental signal to the entire mutant herd. This signal sent the entire herd running for the center of town. Looking out over Seventh and Main the guys quickly realize that they are literally caught in a mutant cattle stampede.

"Holy shit it feels like a damn earthquake out there."

"Look out there guys, the damn things are everywhere."

"Travis, Smalley both of you are two of the best shots that I have ever seen. Travis, I saw you take out a deer at over a thousand yards. Take their damn eyes out. Let's send these bullets directly into their mutated brains."

"We got this Dan."

Dan, Travis, and Smalley all take their perfect aims and begin to take out cow after mutant cow. Dan grabs the beer spout and begins spraying the cattle, stopping them all in their tracks for just a moment. Yet that moment is all that any of the three need to shoot as many of the beasts that they can. Mutant cows' brains and bodies now fill the intersection of Seventh and Main.

"Keep shooting and kill each and every one of these mutant sons of bitches. I have an idea, a big surprise for these mutant freaks."

"Let's make some cheeseburgers out of their asses boys."

"Copy that, Travis."

The guys kill mutant after mutant until it looks as if the herd is finally thinning out. Then for whatever reason, all the mutant cattle stop in their tracks. They begin to scream in unison, the sound loud enough to pop one's eardrums. The guys drop down to their knees and cover their ears with their hands.

"Holy shit make them stop with that damn screaming. I can't fucking take it."

"If I knew how I would Smalley."

"Dan what do you think they are doing?"

"I don't know Travis, but I don't think it's anything good bro."

Finally, almost as soon as they started, the mutant cattle stop their death scream. Out of nowhere a loud bass-filled rumble fills the air. This loud rumble is so deep that it shakes the very building the guys are on top of.

"What the hell is that rumble guys?"

"I don't know Smalley I have never heard or felt anything like this before in my life."

"I don't want to know what the hell this is. All I do know is that it will not be good at all."

"I'm afraid you may be right Travis, but it is too damn late now. I don't know guys, but this may very well be our last stand. I want you both to know that if we don't make it through this you are my brothers, not my friends. No gay, I love you fuckers."

"Same here Dan. We have been brothers since we have been five and six years old."

"Thanks Travis."

"I love you guys but Dan, Travis, we are going to make it through this goddamn it. We are not going to be taken out by a goddamn menu item, it just isn't going to happen. We will not go out like that. Do you fuckers got that?"

The three brothers all give each other a group hug.

"We fucking got this, guys. Smalley is right; nothing that I would throw on my grill is going to take me out. Is it going to take you out Travis?"

"Hell fucking no; let's make us some sloppy Joe's, guys."

"Oh hell no Travis, let's make us some Carne Asada."

Chapter 14:

Just as the guys are about to stop shooting again, they not only hear but feel the ground shake around them. The sound of four massive hooves slam down onto the concrete. All the mutant cattle still alive drop down as if they are bowing or giving reverence. Out from behind the shadows of the Dairy Queen walks the largest Bull to ever walk this planet. The true king of the mutant herd.

The bull steps into view of the streetlight. It's hide is a dark black. The only thing that breaks up the darkness of the hide is the massive muscles and veins running over the entirety of its body. Each of the large veins is glowing neon green, the same color as the mutant blood pumping through its twisted heart. As for muscles, this bull may as well be the Mountain of bulls. Looking at this monster it is hard to see just where the muscles begin and where they end.

The bull's horns must be at least five to six feet long. Yet unlike a normal bull, this mutant son of a bitch has three massive horns on each side. Along with this factor where a normal bull has smooth horns the horns of this bull are all covered with spikes and sharp barbs. If ever even one of these horns were to catch its victim there is no doubt that they would be ripped into pieces.

The fangs, oh the fangs on this abomination of god. The bull's fangs are at least ten to twelve inches long. Each of which is a deep yellow covered in a neon green saliva/goo. As for the size of the beast it stands at least twenty feet tall and is as wide as a Mack truck.

Nothing on this earth has been this large, this evil, or this vicious since the time of the dinosaurs. This may as well be BullZilla. The guys look at each other in utter terror. Never in any of their dreams have the guys ever imagined that anything like this ever could exist, let alone walk the earth. There is a reason that the T-rex was wiped from the earth. There is a reason why the Titans were killed by the gods. This is because there are things that are not supposed to exist in the natural world, let alone the world of men.

"Holy shit look at that damn thing."

"That thing has to be at least five thousand pounds Dan."

"Dan you raise cattle how the hell could anything ever get so damn big?"

"It has to be the green radioactive goo. That same crap that is running through their veins."

"None of that matters now. All that matters is that we kill that damn thing."

"I hear you there Travis. Let's grill this bastard."

The guys unload on the bull, dumping load after load into its skull, and yet the bullets seem to do nothing at all even though they are hitting their mark. All the other cattle are still dropping easily when they shoot them through the eyes. All Dan can think is that the bull must have some sort of protective shield over its eyes and skull.

The monster mutant bull runs full speed, smashing through the entire building. The whole building shakes, now unstable on its foundation. Travis grabs the tap on the keg and sprays beer into his mouth.

"If we are going to die, I am not going to do so sober guys."

"Travis you fucking genius, that is the perfect idea. Smalley help me get this keg."

Dan and Smalley spray the mutant bull in its face with the beer. For just a moment the beast stops, and the two men throw the keg of beer over the side of the building. The keg bounces off the bull's head. Instantly it bites down into the keg with its razor-sharp fangs. The keg erupts filling the bull's belly with nearly fifty gallons of America's finest lager. The massive beast begins to stumble for just a second as it walks towards the intersection of Seventh and Main.

"Look Dan the thing is drunk."

"I wish that we were as well."

"No Travis this is our moment, with the bull drunk and dazed we can kill the damn thing. We may not have long; give me the rocket launcher."

All the mutant cows are now surrounding their mutant god. It's as if they are listening to it speak telepathically. Dan knows that this is his moment to kill the mutant monster. Out of nowhere comes a massive burp from the beast.

"It is full of gas. The moment the rockets hit it the whole damn thing is going to blow. When I shoot, start throwing those damn grenades that you brought, Travis. I want to send this thing back to hell."

Dan takes aim and lets loose, sending all four rockets from the launcher. As they fly through the sky, they remind the guys of mighty fighter jets protecting America. Now it is Dan, Travis, and Smalley protecting America from the complete destruction via mutant cattle. The four missiles smash directly into the side of the Mutant beast, exploding with the force of twenty bombs. The explosion is made even bigger due to the radioactive waste in the beast's blood.

Chunks of mutant flesh falls all over the entire town of Wayne. The guys continue throwing their grenades, killing off the few of the herd that is still alive. The guys have done it. Not only did they kill the lead bull, the god of the herd, Dan, Travis, and Smalley killed the entire mutant herd.

"We did it guys, we killed the entire herd."

"That we did Travis, that we did."

"Dan, Travis, you guys know that we are heroes right?"

"What do we do next Dan?"

"I say that we get some cold beer, something to eat, and then we go check up on those college girls."

"What do you want to eat Dan?"

"Well I know one thing guys, it sure as shit isn't a burger or steak. I'm actually thinking maybe a nice salad."

* 9 7 9 8 6 5 3 3 4 0 6 6 6 *